Mary E. Lyons

ROY MAKES A CAR

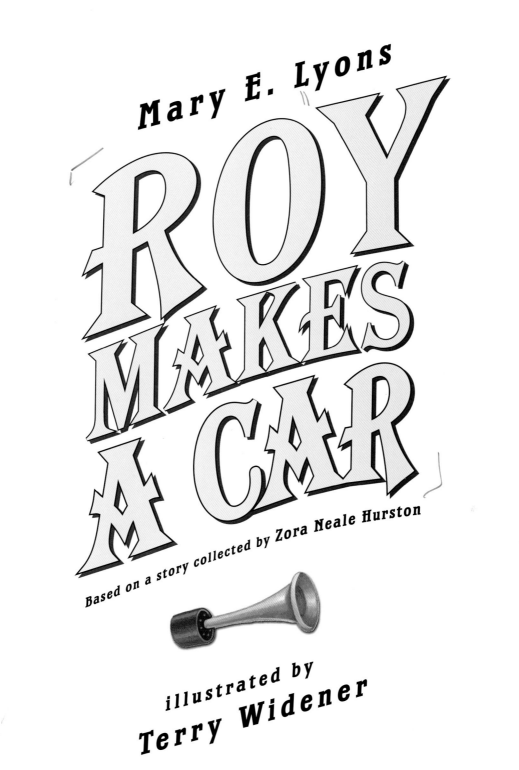

Based on a story collected by Zora Neale Hurston

illustrated by
Terry Widener

Atheneum Books for Young Readers

New York   London   Toronto   Sydney

Dedicated to the floating-ride, stabilated, noncollision

poet Eleanor Ross Taylor,

who first led me to Roy

—M. E. L.

For Joe, who could make anything

—T. W.

A Note About the Text

The original "Roy Makes a Car" is two paragraphs long and belongs to the Library of Congress. Like Hurston, who often recycled and lengthened folklore, I expanded the story. My souped-up version features phrases such as "floating-ride" from magazine advertisements for cars in the 1930s, and dialogue inspired by stories from my southern childhood.

Roy's incredible feats first appeared in print when Stetson Kennedy, a Florida Federal Writers' Project (FWP) editor, compiled *Palmetto Country,* a book of Florida folklore (New York: Duell, Sloan and Pierce, 1942). With Hurston's apparent permission, Kennedy included a three-paragraph version entitled "Roy Sold His Car to God."

Sixty long years after the FWP hired Hurston, her original story was finally published. In the fall of 1998 it appeared in *The Semi-Annual from the University of Virginia,* "Zora Neale Hurston: Unpublished Writings from the Federal Writers' Project: A Special Portfolio," *Meridian,* edited and with an introduction by Pamela Bordelon.

Bordelon's article was a prelude to her book *Go Gator and Muddy the Water: Writings by Zora Neale Hurston from the Federal Writers' Project* (New York: W. W. Norton & Company, 1999). See this book for another copy of the original Roy tale.

To learn more about Hurston and the Florida Federal Writers' Project, visit the Library of Congress Web site at http://memory.loc .gov/ammem/flwpahtml/ffpres01.html.

Other tales collected by Hurston appear in *Raw Head, Bloody Bones: African-American Tales of the Supernatural,* selected by Mary E. Lyons (New York: Scribner, 1991). For a biography of Hurston that weaves her collected folklore with the story of her life, see *Sorrow's Kitchen: The Life and Folklore of Zora Neale Hurston* by Mary E. Lyons (New York: Scribner, 1990). For more information about these and other books by Mary E. Lyons, visit http://www.lyonsdenbooks.com.

Atheneum Books for Young Readers • An imprint of Simon & Schuster Children's Publishing Division • 1230 Avenue of the Americas, New York, New York 10020 • Text copyright © 2005 by Mary E. Lyons • Illustrations copyright © 2005 by Terry Widener • Based on "Florida Folklore: Negro Folk Tales" collected by Zora Neale Hurston in *Florida: A Guide to the Southernmost State,* copyright © 1939; copyright renewed © 1967 by State of Florida Department of Public Instruction • All rights reserved, including the right of reproduction in whole or in part in any form.• Book design by Abelardo Martínez • The text for this book is set in Times New Roman. • The illustrations for this book are rendered in acrylic. • Manufactured in China • First Edition • 10 9 8 7 6 5 4 3 2 1 • Library of Congress Cataloging-in-Publication Data • Lyons, Mary E. • Roy makes a car / Mary E. Lyons ; based on a story collected by Zora Neale Hurston ; illustrated by Terry Widener.—1st ed. • p. cm. • Adapted from a story in *Go Gator and Muddy the Water: Writings by Zora Neale Hurston from the Federal Writers' Project* by Pamela Bordelon (New York: W. W. Norton & Co., 1999) • Summary: Roy Tyle, the best mechanic in the state of Florida, can clean spark plugs just by looking at them, and he takes a two-dollar bet that he can make an accident-proof car. • ISBN 0-689-84640-1 • [1. Folklore—United States. 2. African Americans—Folklore. 3. Tall tales.] I. Hurston, Zora Neale. II. Widener, Terry, ill. III. Title. • PZ8.1.L986Ro 2005 • 398.2—dc22 • 2004003221

Roy Tyle runs the garage down near Eatonville, Florida. Eatonville . . .

now, that's somewhere west of Christmas and north of Boogy's Corner.

People from those parts think Roy Tyle is the best mechanic in the state.

Maybe even the world. Why, he can grease an axle faster than you can say

"carburetor," and he can clean spark plugs just by looking at them hard.

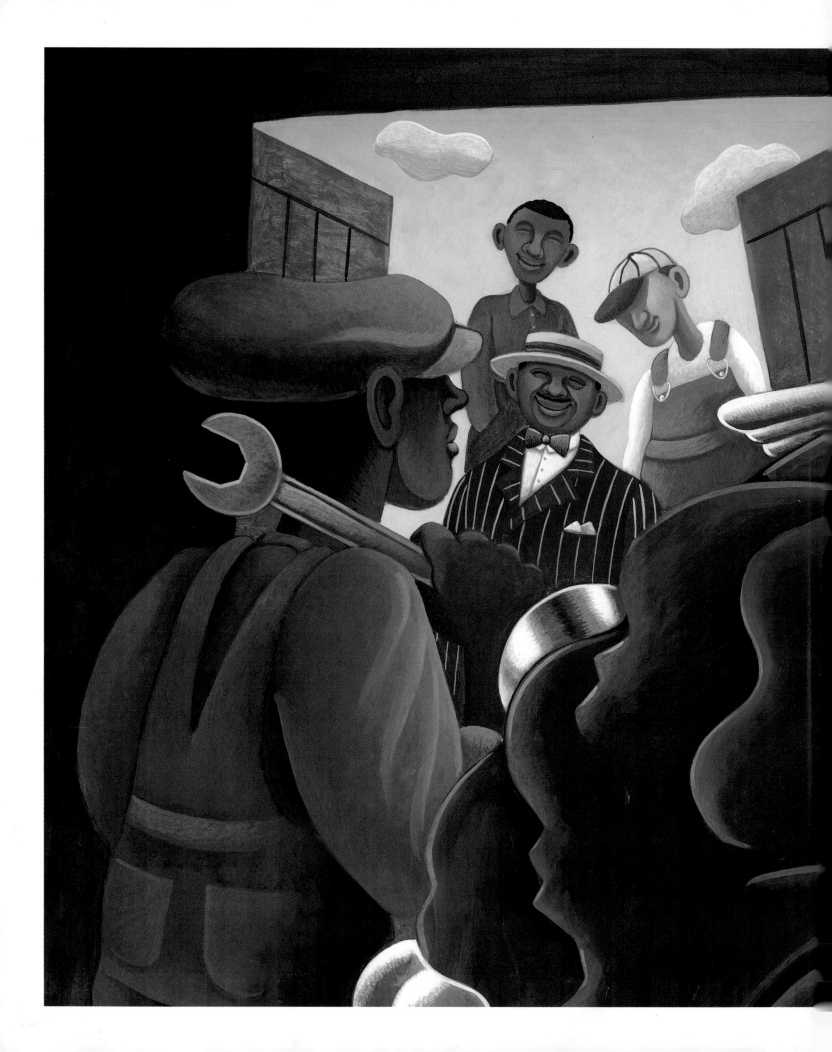

But Roy, you know, he never could find an automobile nowhere made to suit him. Those factory models were always running into one another on the curve of the road. He thought if a car was built right, there wouldn't be none of these collisions. So one day he said he was going to make an accident-proof car.

Roy's neighbors snickered. "Huh! We like you, Roy, but that's a big old lie. How you going to stop accidents?"

Roy answered, "Give me time. I'll show you them crack-ups ain't nothing but foolishness."

That very day Roy locked himself in his garage, set out all his working tools, and got to work. After an hour or so, he told the people he was ready to show his turbocharged, floating-ride, stabilated, lubricated, banjo-axled, wing-fendered, low-compression, noncollision car.

Nobody believed him, so Roy rolled that thing out and stood there grinning, all proud like he just grew a baby. A few folks walked around and kicked all four tires. A couple of snoops lifted the hood and muttered "Hmmmm."

But mostly nobody said much on account of their mouths were hanging open. All this time, and Roy's automobile looked like any other car.

That's when a gambling man laid a bet on Roy Tyle.

"Get in your car, Roy," the man said, growling. "I got two bucks says it can't do diddly out on the road."

So Roy put on goggles and a work cap that told the world, "If Roy Can't Build It, Nobody Can." The people brought out one car and then another to meet him on the curve.

The first was an eight-cylinder, free-wheeling Chrysler roadster. Roy's car buzzed around that thing like a bee on a coconut cake. Then they cranked up a master-six-cylinder Chevrolet sedan with a one-piece turret top.

"Move out the way!" Roy hollered as he pulled the choke and lifted the throttle. His cap sailed up . . .

. . . and landed in Georgia—where folks are wondering to this day, who the heck is Roy?—and his goggles corkscrewed clean over to Alabama. Meantime, Roy's car cruised right over the Chevy's solid steel roof.

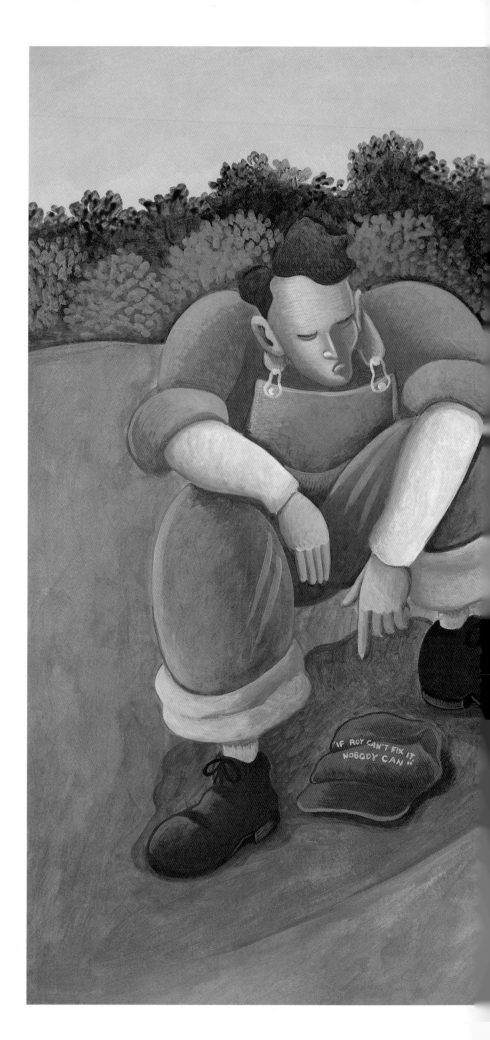

"Let's try a Mack truck!" somebody shouted. But when the truck rounded the corner, Roy pressed a special button on his dash and ran smack under it. You just couldn't hit Roy Tyle.

Well, the gambling man knew he was fixing to lose his bet, so he went and got his Roadmaster Buick. Now, a Buick is so underslung and low to the ground that it looks like it's squatting down all the time. And this man said Roy's car couldn't squat under no Buick.

But it sure did. It slid right under the sealed chassis, past the tiptoe hydraulic brakes, and shot out square between the rear power-float tires.

The gambling man was awful put out about the whole business. He coughed up the two dollars, though.

"Hey, Roy!" somebody shouted. "You've made yourself a fine machine."

"Yeah!" yelled somebody else. "So fine maybe you could get cash for it."

Roy thought they might be right. The next day he took his car up to Boogy's Corner, sold it off for a bundle, and came on back home.

Way after a while, Roy got tired of just sitting around the place. He claimed he felt too lonesome without something to ride in.

That's when Roy told his wife, "I believe I'm going to make myself another car."

This time he took and made a car that had flaps folded on top of it. That way he could just flip the flaps and zoom around curves so things couldn't hit him.

Well, from flying his car around them curves, he took to flying it right smart. Finally he didn't drive on the ground hardly at all. And that's just how he got rid of the second car.

One day, you see, Roy was way up in the sky, dipping-the-dip. He didn't know it, but God was sitting in heaven's bleachers, spying on him. Seen that automobile and liked it so much that He waved Roy over.

God whipped out His money and bought Roy's car on the spot.

And before you know it, God was out making some cars just like it for the angels. Ever since, them angels ain't flew a lick with their own wings. They're all driving around heaven in brand-new Roy-mobiles.

At first Roy was sort of sorry he'd sold his car to God. But you know Roy. He's back home cooking up something else. It must be a doozy, because he's got a lock the size of Miami on those double doors.

A few nosy people have walked by the garage a time or two. One woman swears she's seen the walls sqooshing in and out. Told her husband something in there sounded like a cross between a locomotive and a tractor.

The husband said, naw, he's seen the roof whump up a few feet. He's pretty sure Roy's working on a propeller chain saw.

And the gambling man claims that Roy's new machine is nothing but a flat-footed fake. Some folks never do wise up.

If you've got the time, drop by Roy's garage and see for yourself.

But don't stand too close! That Roy Tyle is a wonder-making man.

'Tain't no telling what he'll try next.

AUTHOR'S NOTE

Zora Neale Hurston (1891–1960) was an African-American anthropologist, folklorist, and writer. One of the greatest story catchers of the twentieth century, she published African-American folkways in three collections of folklore, three novels, and an autobiography. Though book critics praised Hurston's rare ability to capture southern African-American speech, many of her collected folktales were unpublished during her lifetime. The original version of "Roy Makes a Car" was one of them.

How Hurston caught Roy's story is a story all its own. In 1936, during the Great Depression, the U.S. government started the Federal Writers' Project (FWP). States received federal money and paid writers to gather information for state tourist guides. Each guidebook included maps, suggestions for car trips, and folk customs from throughout the state.

By 1938 the Florida FWP office faced a problem. They had hired inexperienced writers, and the collected material needed the expert eye of an editor. The national FWP office in Washington, D.C., recommended that Hurston organize the Florida book. They also wanted her to add any new folklore she was collecting herself.

Hurston was the perfect choice, because no one knew southern African-American folklore better than she. Raised in the all-black town of Eatonville, Florida, she was surrounded as a child by tales and no end of folks to tell them. Although she left the state as a teenager, she never forgot how humorous stories helped Florida's African Americans cope with dangerous, slavelike working conditions. Turpentine workers and orange pickers were more than faceless laborers to Hurston. They were her people, and their tales—told in rich dialect with African origins and laced with wisdom and humor—were jewels to be saved.

In need of money, Hurston applied for the FWP job. Despite the endorsement from Washington, the Florida office refused to pay her an editor's wages because she was black. Ignoring the discrimination, she accepted a lower salary, moved back to Eatonville, and polished the text for *Florida: A Guide to the Southernmost State.*

As requested, Hurston added folktales she had collected, including "Roy Makes a Car." No one knows where or when she heard about Roy, but she had a knack for pulling stories out of people. Maybe she was sitting on someone's front porch when she caught a scrap of idle talk about a man who could make anything. She may have asked to hear more, and a story was born.

We don't know if Hurston flavored "Roy Makes a Car" with her own words. It hardly matters, because southern African-American folklore was in her bones. And we'll never know why editors in the Washington FWP office who compiled the final version of the Florida guide deleted Roy's tale. Perhaps a story about cars sounded too modern to them.

Luckily Hurston knew good folklore when she heard it. She had already caught other African-American tall tales about Uncle Monday, an alligator that turned into a man every Monday; Big John the Conqueror, a slave who could outsmart "Ole Massa"; and Big Sixteen, a fellow so large that he wore a size sixteen shoe. With Roy, Hurston found yet another hero who kept the people, as she once wrote, "laughing with their mouths wide open."